The Princess Who Never Smiled

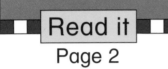

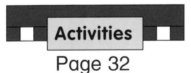

"What are we going to do with the princess?" asked the king. "She is never happy."

So the king and queen wrote a letter
and sent it across the land.

The letter said: "He who makes the princess smile will become her prince."

So, from east to west and from north to south, lines formed to see the princess.

A clown was first. "Did you ever see a pie fly?" he asked. The clown threw a pie into the air, and it landed on his head! But the princess didn't smile.

A cowboy was second. "Howdy, partner," he said. The cowboy rode upside-down on his horse in his underwear! But the princess didn't smile.

A magician was third. "Abracadabra," he said. Then he pulled a huge elephant out of his hat! But the princess didn't smile.

"No one can make the princess smile," cried the king and queen. But at that very moment, the royal chef came in, balancing a huge tray of food, and . . .

… the chef tripped over the rug, the tray went flying, and the food landed—*splat*—on top of the king and queen!

A big smile broke over the princess's face. She laughed loud enough for the whole kingdom to hear. And the princess lived happily ever after with her new prince … and she always had delicious food to eat!

Write it

Look at the picture on each page, and then write the story in your own words.

_____

_____

_____

_____

_____

_____

_____

_____

_____

_____

_____

_____

_____

_____

_____

_____

_____

Write it

Write it

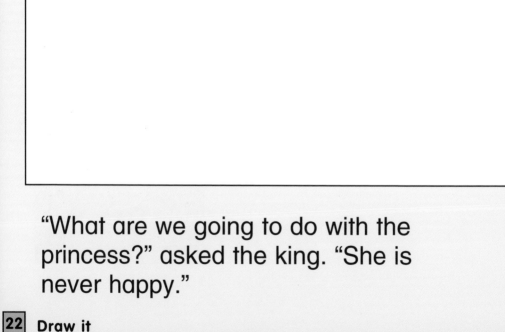

"What are we going to do with the princess?" asked the king. "She is never happy."

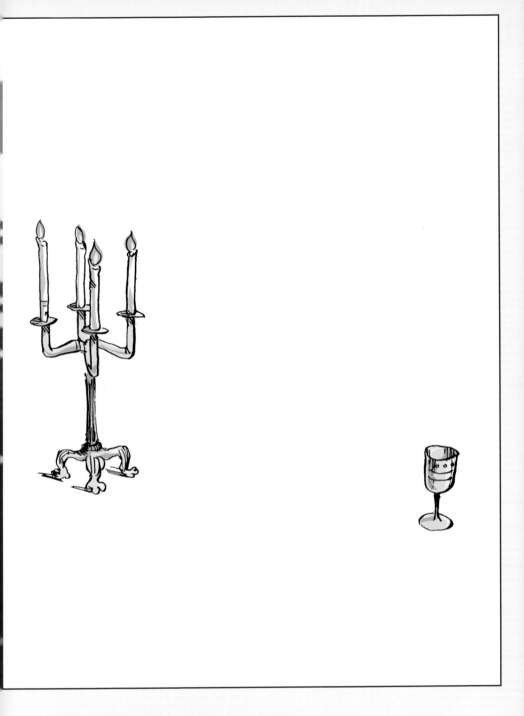

So the king and queen wrote a letter
and sent it across the land.

The letter said: "He who makes the
princess smile will become her prince."

Draw it

So, from east to west and from north to south, lines formed to see the princess.

A clown was first. "Did you ever see a pie fly?" he asked. The clown threw a pie into the air, and it landed on his head! But the princess didn't smile.

Draw it

A cowboy was second. "Howdy, partner," he said. The cowboy rode upside-down on his horse in his underwear! But the princess didn't smile.

A magician was third. "Abracadabra," he said. Then he pulled a huge elephant out of his hat! But the princess didn't smile.

Draw it

"No one can make the princess smile," cried the king and queen. But at that very moment, the royal chef came in, balancing a huge tray of food, and . . .

... the chef tripped over the rug, the tray went flying, and the food landed—*splat*—on top of the king and queen!

A big smile broke over the princess's face. She laughed loud enough for the whole kingdom to hear. And the princess lived happily ever after with her new prince ... and she always had delicious food to eat!

Activities

Read it:

Use a funny voice! Have your child or student select a story from a Now I'm Reading!™ book. He or she should practice reading the story using different expressive voices. For example, he or she could read the story with an opera singer voice, a whisper voice, a loud voice, a cowboy voice, a robot voice, and so on. Your child or student quickly will become a master at reading that story. You can even record the story for him or her for extra laughs!

Write it:

Interview a family member or friend! Interviews are a super fun way to learn more about someone and to practice writing. First, have your child or student choose a person to interview. Next, he or she should write a list of five or more questions to ask that person. Remind him or her to leave enough space below each question to write the answer. Ask your child or student to share the interview questions and answers with others. He or she can even staple various interviews together to create a book.

Draw it:

Make a map! Have your child or student draw a map of a specific room in his or her home. He or she should sit in the room with his or her paper and pencil and really think about the layout of the room and the items in it. He or she should think about where things are and the amount of space between things. Instruct your child or student to try to draw the little details as well as the bigger items. He or she can also label the items on the map and use colors that are representative of the room. As an extra challenge, your child or student can draw maps of additional rooms to create a big book of maps!

A NOTE TO PARENTS:
When children create their own spellings for words they don't know, they are using **inventive spelling**. For the beginner, the act of writing is more important than the correctness of form. Sounding out words and predicting how they will be spelled reinforces an understanding of the connection between letters and sounds. Eventually, through experimenting with spelling patterns and repeated exposure to standard spelling, children will learn and use the correct form in their own writing. Until then, inventive spelling encourages early experimentation and self-expression in writing and nurtures a child's confidence as a writer.